To the square pegs

Tundra Books, an imprint of Penguin Random House Canada Young Readers,
a division of Penguin Random House of Canada Limited

Library and Archives Canada Cataloguing in Publication

Title: Thingamabob / Marianna Coppo.
Names: Coppo, Marianna, author, illustrator.
Identifiers: Canadiana (print) 20200361848 | Canadiana (ebook) 20200361856
ISBN 9780735265790 (hardcover) | ISBN 9780735265806 (EPUB)
Classification: LCC PZ7.1.C66 Thi 2021 | DDC j813/.6—dc23

Published simultaneously in the United States of America by Tundra Books of
Northern New York, an imprint of Penguin Random House Canada Young Readers,
a division of Penguin Random House of Canada Limited

Library of Congress Control Number: 2020947869

Edited by Peter Phillips
Acquired by Tara Walker
Translated by Debbie Bibo
Designed by John Martz
The artwork in this book was rendered in tempera, pastels and digital collage.
The text was set in Helvetica Rounded.

Printed in China

www.penguinrandomhouse.ca

1 2 3 4 5   25 24 23 22 21

tundra | Penguin Random House | TUNDRA BOOKS

Marianna Coppo

Thingamabob

tundra

In the beginning, the universe was
one great big thing.

**Then, in an instant,
the thing exploded into gobs and
gobs of thingamabobs.**

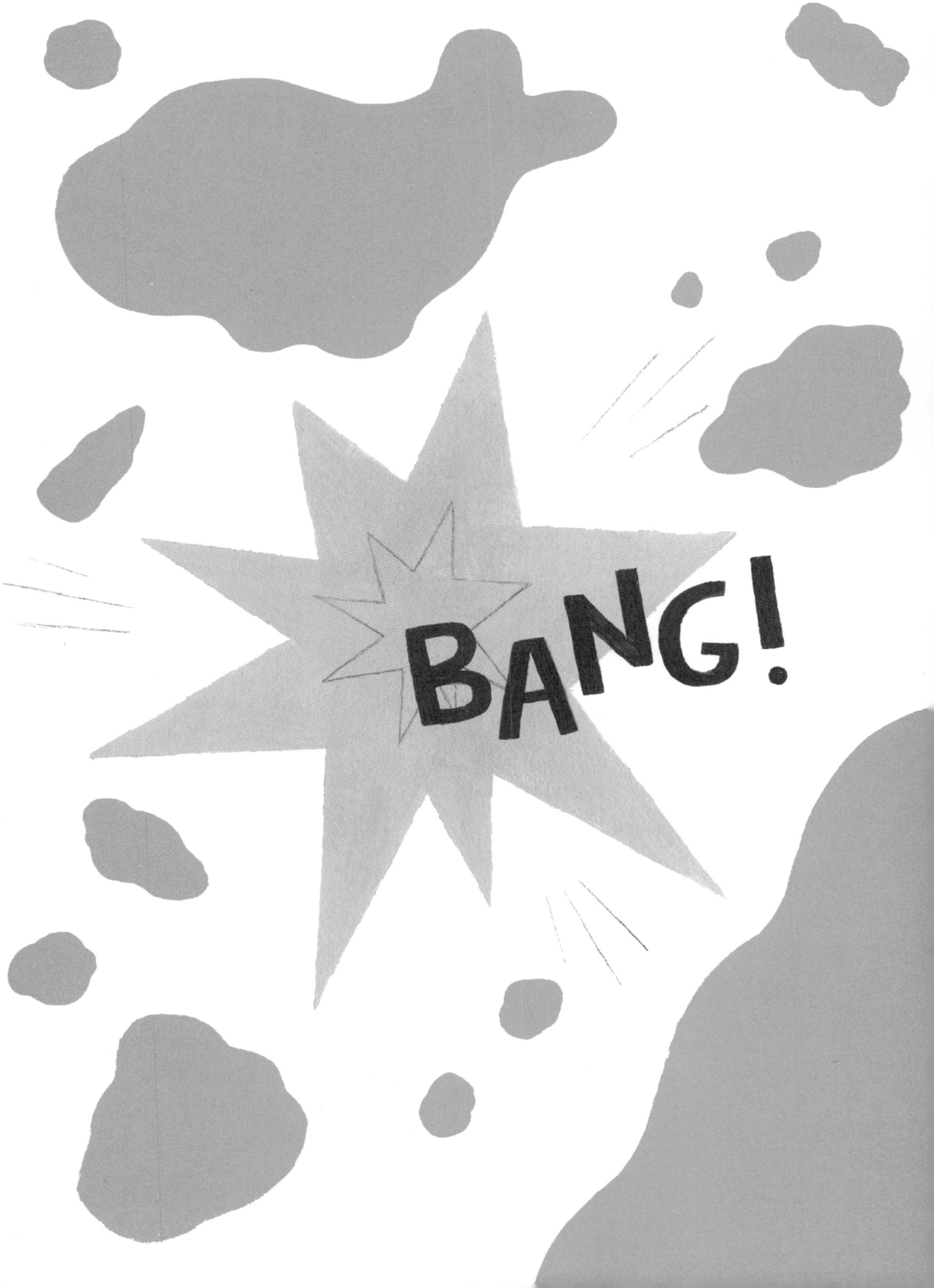
BANG!

One by one, the thingamabobs
became all of the things
we know today . . .

big things,
little things
and even very
complicated things.

Everything was in its place.

Well, everything except for one small, shapeless thingamabob.

No one knew what it was.

And no one was clear what it was for.

It wasn't comfortable enough

or frightening enough

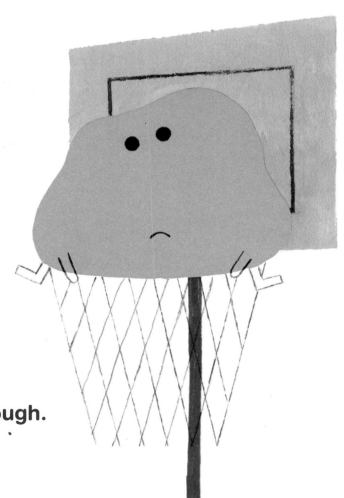

or round enough.

It wasn't sweet enough

or fashionable
enough

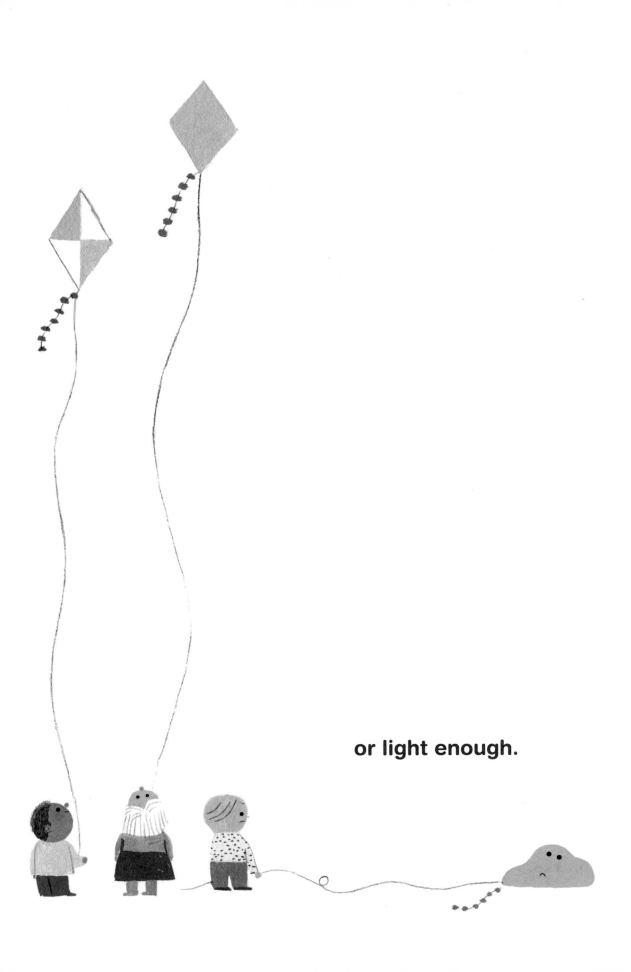

or light enough.

It wasn't this or that.
It wasn't here or there.

What's the use of this thingamabob?

"Hey!"

**That day, Thingamabob was
many things . . .**

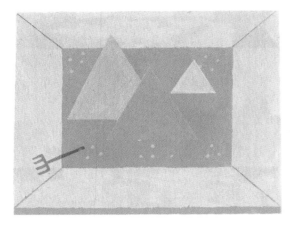

. . . especially a friend.

PLINK

**Thingamabob realized that being a thingamabob
was actually pretty good.**

Because if you aren't one thing . . .

. . . you can be anything.